Contents

A Paper Doll's House

An extract from *Marjorie's Vacation*
by Carolyn Wells

Marjorie is stuck in bed with a sprained ankle, but her good friend Molly has come over to play with her. They have another friend, Stella, whom they find rather quiet.

MOLLY HAD BROUGHT OVER her paper doll's house. It was quite different from anything Marjorie had ever seen before, so she wondered if she couldn't make one for herself.

A Surprise Party

and other toy stories

Compiled by Tig Thomas

First published in 2014 by Miles Kelly Publishing Ltd
Harding's Barn, Bardfield End Green, Thaxted, Essex, CM6 3PX, UK

2 4 6 8 10 9 7 5 3 1

Publishing Director Belinda Gallagher
Creative Director Jo Cowan
Editorial Director Rosie Neave
Senior Editor Sarah Parkin
Senior Designer Joe Jones
Production Manager Elizabeth Collins
Reprographics Stephan Davis, Jennifer Hunt, Thom Allaway

ISBN 978-1-78209-467-8

Printed in China

British Library Cataloguing-in-Publication Data
A catalogue record for this book is available from the British Library

ACKNOWLEDGEMENTS

The publishers would like to thank the following artists who have contributed to this book:

Advocate Art: Claire Keay, Bruno Merz (inc. cover), Kimberley Scott
Beehive Illustration: Rupert Van Wyk (inc. decorative frames)

Made with paper from a sustainable forest

www.mileskelly.net   info@mileskelly.net

A paper doll's house is quite different from the other kind of doll's house, and Molly's was made of a large blank book.

So Uncle Steve bought a book almost exactly like it for Marjorie, and then he bought her scissors, glue and several catalogues. He also bought her a pile of magazines and papers, which were crammed full of advertisements.

The two little girls set busily to work, and soon they had cut out a quantity of chairs, tables, beds and furniture from the pictured pages. These they pasted in the book. Each of the pages was a room, and in the room were arranged furniture and ornaments.

The parlour had beautiful tables and chairs, rugs, pictures, ornaments and even

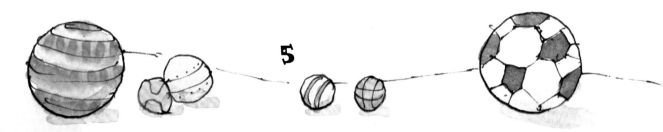

lace curtains at the windows. The dining room was fully furnished, and the kitchen contained everything a cook might need. The bedrooms were beautiful with dainty beds and dressing tables.

In addition, there were halls, a nursery, playroom, and pleasant verandas fitted up with hammocks and porch furniture.

Of course it required some imagination to think that these rooms were in the shape of a house, and not just pages in a book, but both Marjorie and Molly had plenty of imagination. Besides, it was fun to cut out the things and arrange them in their places.

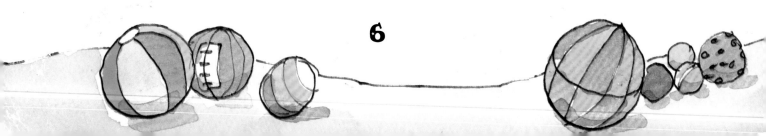

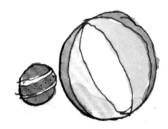

The family for the paper doll's house was selected from clothes catalogues. Charming ladies and children of all ages were found in plenty. Hats and parasols were cut out, which could be neatly put away in the cupboards and wardrobes that were in the house. Marjorie had discovered that by pasting only the edges of the wardrobe and carefully cutting the doors apart, they could be made to open and shut beautifully.

Every morning Molly would come over and they played with their paper doll's houses. Each girl added a second book,

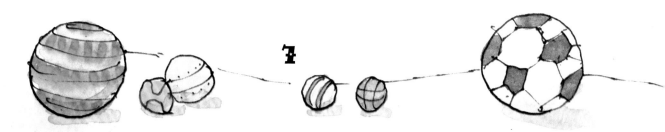

which represented grounds and gardens. There were fountains and flowerbeds and trees and shrubs, which they cut from florists' catalogues.

One day, Grandma told Marjorie that she would invite both Stella and Molly to come to tea from four until five o' clock.

The little girls were glad to meet again. They showed Stella their paper doll's houses. Stella was an expert at paper dolls, and knew how to draw and cut out lovely dolls. She told Marjorie that if she had a paintbox she could paint them.

"I wish you would come over some other day, Stella, and do it," said Marjorie. "I know Uncle Steve will get me a paintbox if I ask him to. We'll have lots of fun, won't we?"

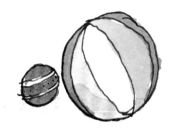

"Yes, thank you," said Stella quietly.

At last Jane came in with the tea tray, and at the sight of the crackers and milk, the strawberries and little cakes, Marjorie braced herself up on her pillows and Molly, who was sitting on the bed, bounced up and down with glee.

Molly and Marjorie enjoyed the good things, as they always enjoyed everything. But Stella sat holding a plate in one hand and a glass of milk in the other, and showed about as much excitement as a marble statue. Somehow the whole look of the child was too much for Marjorie's spirit of mischief.

Suddenly, and in a loud voice, she said to Stella, "Boo!"

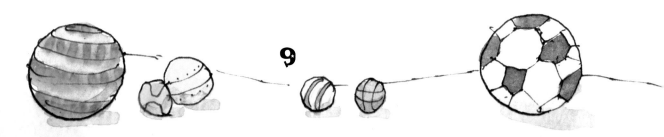

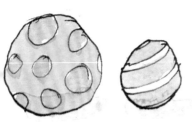

This, in itself, was not frightful, but coming so unexpectedly it startled Stella. She jumped, her glass and plate fell to the floor with a crash, and strawberries, cakes and milk fell.

Frightened and nervous at the whole affair, Stella began to cry. Into this distracting scene came Grandma. She stood looking in amazement at the three children and the debris on the floor.

"It's my fault, Grandma," Marjorie said. "I scared Stella. She couldn't help dropping her things."

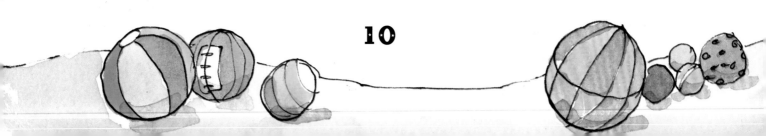

"You are a naughty girl, Marjorie," said Grandma, as she tried to comfort Stella.

"I'm awfully sorry," said Marjorie. "Please forgive me, Stella. But honestly I didn't think it would scare you so. What would you do, Molly, if I said 'boo' to you?"

"I'd say 'boo yourself'!" said Molly.

"I know you would," said Marjorie, "but you see Stella's different, and I ought to have remembered. Don't cry, Stella, truly I'm sorry! Don't cry, and I'll give you my – my paper doll's house."

"I won't take it," Stella said, "It wasn't your fault. I oughtn't to have been so silly as to be scared because you said 'boo'."

But Stella, though she had quite forgiven Marjorie, was upset by the whole affair and

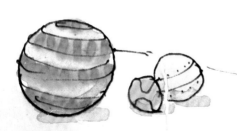
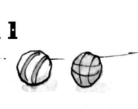

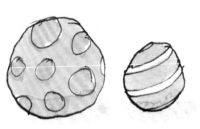

wanted to go home.

So Marjorie was left alone to think, and half an hour later Grandma returned.

"That was a naughty trick, Marjorie," Grandma said.

"I was mischievous, but truly, she did look so stiff – I just had to make her jump."

"I know what you mean, Marjorie, but I want you to grow up polite and kind. You knew it wasn't kind to make Stella jump."

"No, I know it wasn't, Grandma, and I'm sorry now," Marjorie said. "But whenever Stella comes over again, I'll be very kind to her, to make up for saying 'boo'."

A Surprise Party

An extract from *Little Men*
by Louisa May Alcott

*Aunt Jo (also called Mrs Bhaer) runs a school for boys,
including her nephew Demi, and two boys called Tommy and Nat.
It also has a few girls – her niece, Demi's twin, Daisy, a tomboy
called Nan and Daisy's cousin, Bess.*

"**PLEASE, AUNT JO,** would you and the girls come out to a surprise party we have made for you? Do, it's a very nice one."

"Thank you, we will come with pleasure. Only, I must take Teddy with me," replied

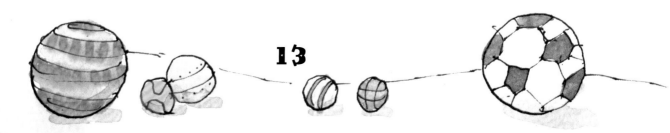

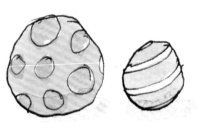

Aunt Jo, with a smile.

"We'd like to have him. The little wagon is all ready for the girls. You won't mind walking just up to Pennyroyal Hill, will you Aunt Jo?"

"Thank you kindly, sir," and Aunt Jo made him a grand curtsey.

Everyone bustled about, and in five minutes the three little girls and Teddy were packed into the clothes basket, as they called the wicker wagon, which Toby drew.

Demi walked at the head of the procession, and Aunt Jo brought up the rear. The three girls had little flutters of excitement all the way there, and Teddy was so charmed with the drive that he kept dropping his little hat overboard.

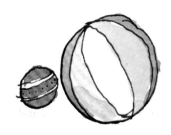

When they came to the hill 'nothing was to be seen but the grass blowing in the wind,' as the fairy books say, and they all looked disappointed. But Demi said, "Now, you all get out and stand still, and the surprise party will come to you."

A short pause of intense suspense, and then Nat, Demi and Tommy marched forth from behind a rock, each bearing a new kite, which they presented to the three girls. Shrieks of delight arose, but were silenced by the boys, who said, "That isn't all the surprise." And, running behind the rock, they emerged again bearing a fourth kite of superb size, on which was printed, in bright yellow letters, 'For Mother Bhaer'.

"We thought you'd like one, too," cried

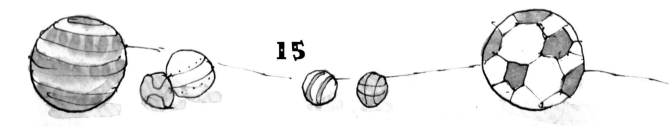

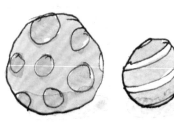

all three boys, shaking with laughter.

Aunt Jo clapped her hands and joined in the laugh.

"These are magnificent kites. We were wishing we had some the other day, when you were flying yours, weren't we, girls?" Aunt Jo said.

"That's why we made them for you," cried Tommy.

"Let us fly them," said energetic Nan.

"I don't know how," began Daisy.

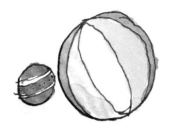

"We'll show you!" cried all the boys, as Demi took Daisy's, Tommy took Nan's, and Nat, with difficulty, persuaded Bess to let go of her little blue one.

"Aunty, if you will wait a minute, we'll pitch yours for you," said Demi.

"Bless your buttons, dear. I know all about it. And here is a boy who will toss it up for me," added Aunt Jo, as the professor peeped over the rock with a face full of fun.

He came out at once, tossed up the big kite, and Aunt Jo ran off with it in fine style, while the children stood and enjoyed the spectacle. One by one all the kites went up and floated far overhead like birds, balancing themselves on the fresh breeze that blew steadily over the hill.

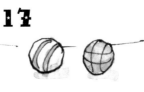

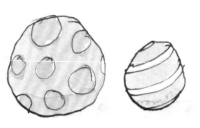

Such a merry time they had! Running and shouting, sending up the kites or pulling them down, feeling them tug at the string like live creatures trying to escape.

Nan was quite wild with the fun. Daisy thought the new play nearly as interesting as dolls. Little Bess was so fond of her kite that she would only let it go on very short flights, preferring to hold it in her lap. And Aunt Jo enjoyed her kite immensely.

Eventually everyone got tired, and fastening the kite strings to trees and fences, all sat down to rest.

"Did you ever have such a good time as this before?" asked Nat.

"Not since I last flew a kite, years ago, when I was a girl," answered Aunt Jo.

"Tell us about the last time you flew a kite," said Nat.

"I was a girl of fifteen, and was ashamed to be seen at such a play. So Uncle Teddy and I privately made our kites, and stole away to fly them. We had a capital time, and were resting as we are now, when suddenly we heard voices, and saw a party of young ladies and gentlemen coming back from a picnic. Teddy did not mind, although he was rather a large boy to be playing with a kite. But I was in a great flurry, for I knew I should be sadly laughed at and never hear the last of it.

"'What shall I do?' I whispered to Teddy, as the voices drew nearer and nearer.

"'I'll show you,' he said, and whipping

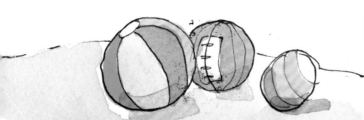

out his knife he cut the strings. Away flew the kites, and when the people came up we were picking flowers as properly as you please. They never suspected us, and we had a grand laugh over our narrow escape."

"Were the kites lost?" asked Daisy.

"Quite lost," said Aunt Jo, beginning to pull in the big kite, for it was getting late.

"Must we go now?"

"I must, or you won't have any supper!" Aunt Jo replied.

"Hasn't our party been a nice one?" asked Tommy.

"Splendid!" answered everyone.

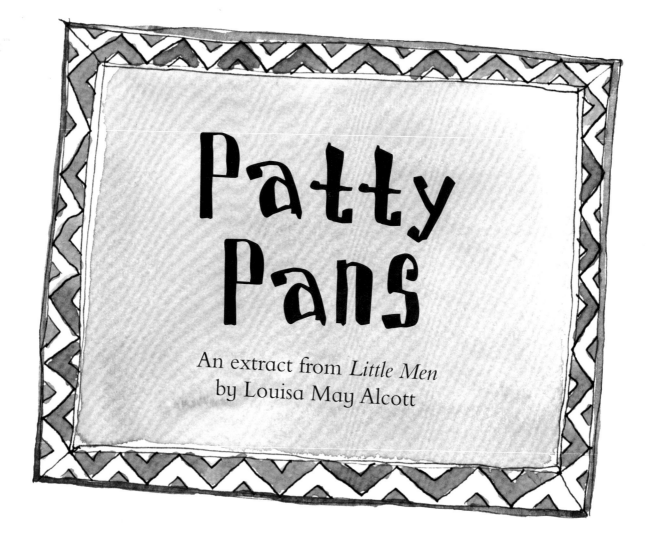

Patty Pans

An extract from *Little Men*
by Louisa May Alcott

Aunt Jo (also called Mrs Bhaer) runs a school for boys and looks after her niece, Daisy. She also has a little boy called Teddy, named after his Uncle Teddy.

"**WHAT'S THE MATTER, DAISY?**" asked Aunt Jo.

"I'm tired of playing alone!" Daisy said.

"I'll play with you later, but just now I must get ready for a trip into town. What

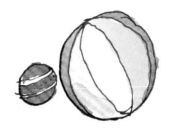

will you do with yourself while I go?"

"I don't know. I'm tired of dolls. I wish you'd make up a new play for me, Aunt Jo," said Daisy.

"I shall have to think of a brand new one, so suppose you go down and see what Asia has got for your lunch," suggested Aunt Jo.

Daisy ran off, and Aunt Jo racked her brain for a new play for her. All of a sudden she seemed to have an idea, for she smiled to herself.

What it was no one found out that day, but Aunt Jo's eyes twinkled when she told Daisy she had thought of a new play, and that she had bought it.

Daisy was very excited and said, "How

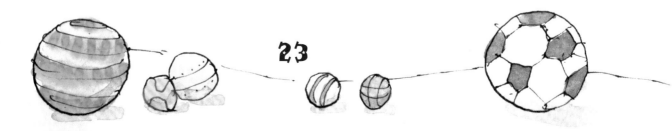

can I wait so long? Couldn't I see it today?"

"Oh dear, no! It has got to be arranged. I promised Uncle Teddy that you shouldn't see it until it was all in order."

"If Uncle knows about it then it must be splendid!" cried Daisy.

"Yes, Uncle Teddy went and bought it with me, and we had such fun in the shop choosing the different parts. You must give him your best kiss when he comes, for he is the kindest uncle that ever went and bought a charming little coo – Bless me! I nearly told you what it was!" and Aunt Jo cut herself off in the middle. Then Daisy sat quite still, trying to think what play had a 'coo' in it.

Daisy got through the afternoon, went to

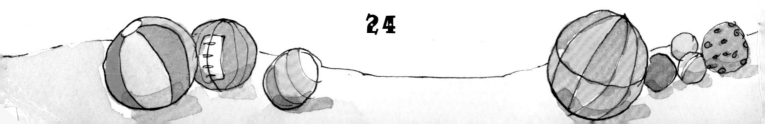

bed early, and next morning went to see her Aunt Jo to have the new play.

"It's all ready, come on," said Aunt Jo, and she led the way upstairs to the nursery.

"I don't see anything," said Daisy.

"Do you hear anything?" asked Aunt Jo.

Daisy did hear an odd crackling, and then a little sound as of a kettle singing. These noises came from behind a curtain drawn before a deep bay window. Daisy snatched it back quickly, gave one joyful "Oh!" and then stood gazing at, what do you think?

A wide seat ran around the three sides of the window. On one side hung little pots and pans, on the other side there was a small dinner and tea set, and in the middle

part a cooking stove, a real stove, big
enough to cook for a large family of very
hungry dolls. But the best of it was that a
real fire burned in it. Just above the stove
hung a dustpan and brush, a little market
basket was on the low table, and over the
back of a little chair hung a white apron.

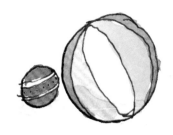

Daisy stood still after the first glad 'Oh!' Then the happy little girl hugged her Aunt Jo, saying gratefully, "Oh Aunty, it's a splendid new play! It's the sweetest, dearest kitchen in the world. Can I learn pies, and cake, and macaroni, and everything?"

"All in good time. I thought I'd see if I could find a little stove for you, and teach you to cook. That would be fun, and useful too. I shall tell you what to do and show you how."

"Oh, what shall I do first?" asked Daisy.

"Shut the stove, so that the oven may heat up. Then wash your hands and get out the flour, sugar, salt, butter and cinnamon. See if the pie board is clean, and then peel your apple ready to put in."

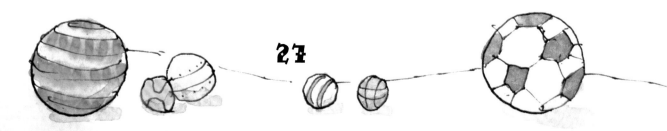

Daisy got things together with as little noise and spilling as could be expected from so young a cook.

"Take that little pan full of flour and then rub in as much butter as will go on that plate," Aunt Jo said.

"I know how. Don't I butter the pie plates as well?" asked Daisy, whisking the flour about.

"Quite right! I do believe you have a gift for cooking," said Aunt Jo, approvingly. "Now scatter some flour on the board and roll the pastry out – yes, that's the way."

Daisy rolled and rolled with the little pin and, having got her pastry, covered the plates with it. Next the apple was sliced in, sugar and cinnamon sprinkled over it, and

then the top crust was put on.

"I always wanted to cut them round. How nice it is to do it all by myself!" said Daisy, as the little knife went clipping round the doll's pie plate poised on her hand.

"Now I put them in!" she said, and she shut the pies in the little oven.

"Clear up your things," Aunt Jo said. "Then peel your squash and potatoes. Cut the potatoes up, so they will go into the little pot. Then put on your vegetables, set the table, and get ready to cook the steak."

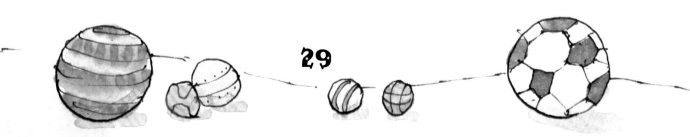

What a thing it was to see the potatoes bobbing about in the little pot, to peep at the squash getting soft so fast in the tiny steamer, to whisk open the oven door every five minutes to see how the pies got on, and to put two real steaks in a tiny pan, then proudly turn them with a fork.

The potatoes were done first. They were pounded up with a little pestle, had much butter put in, then put in the oven to brown.

So interested had Daisy been, that she forgot her pastry until she opened the oven door to put in the potato. Then a wail arose, for alas! The little pies were burned black!

"Oh, my pies! My darling pies! They are all spoilt!" cried poor Daisy.

"Dear, dear, I forgot to remind you to

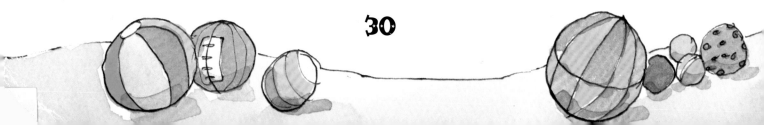

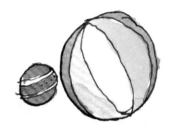

take them out," said Aunt Jo. "Don't cry, darling, we'll try again after dinner," she added, as a tear dropped from Daisy's eye and sizzled on the hot ruins of a pie.

"Put the meat dish and your own plates down to warm, while you mash the squash with butter, salt, and a little pepper on the top," said Aunt Jo, hoping that the dinner would meet with no further disasters.

The dinner was safely put upon the table, the six dolls were seated three on a side, Teddy took the bottom, and Daisy the top. One doll was in full ball costume, another in her nightgown. Jerry, the boy, wore his red winter suit, while Annabella was dressed in nothing but her own skin.

Teddy, as father of the family, smilingly

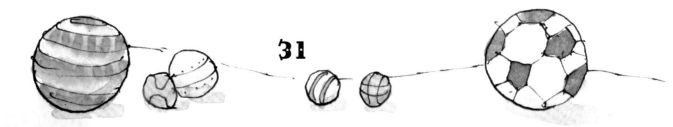

ate everything offered to him, and did not find a single fault. The steak was so tough that the little carving knife would not cut it, the potato did not go round, and the squash was very lumpy, but the master and mistress of the house cleared the table.

"That is the nicest lunch I ever had. Can't I do it every day?" asked Daisy, as she scraped up and ate the leavings.

"You can cook things every day after lessons," said Aunt Jo.

"It is the dearest play ever made!" cried Daisy. "I just wish everybody had a sweet cooking stove like mine."

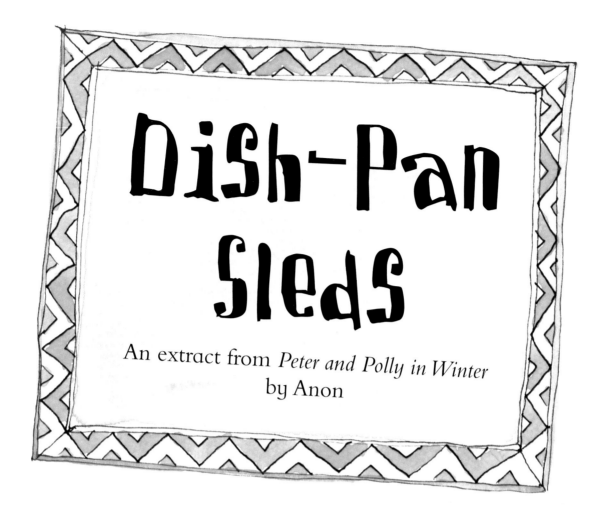

Dish-Pan Sleds

An extract from *Peter and Polly in Winter*
by Anon

Peter and Polly live on a farm, which gets deep snow in winter.

"**P**ETER AND POLLY, would you like to play a new game?" asked Mother.

"Oh, yes, oh, yes! What is it?" cried both children excitedly.

"I can't tell you," said Mother. "But I'll show you. Get ready to go out of doors.

Here comes Tim – he can play too."

"How many can be in this game, Mother?" Polly asked.

"Ever so many, Polly. Please take this dish pan. Peter, carry this pan. Tim, here is one for you. Now follow me."

Mrs Howe went through the open gate into the top of the hayfield. There was a hard crust on the top of the snow.

"Look children," Mother said. "What a fine, icy crust. It holds me up and it's just right for sliding. Before long the sun will make it soft."

"I wish we had our sleds," said Peter. "Let's go back for them."

"You have them with you," said Mother. "That is the game."

"I don't see any sleds," said Peter.

"Then I will show you. Bring your big pan here and put it down on the edge of the hill. Now sit in it and hold onto the handles. Keep your feet up. You don't need to steer — you can't run into anything here."

Mother gave Peter a push, and away he went on the icy crust.

"Mother!" cried Polly, jumping up and down. "Look at Peter! I want to go!"

"In a minute," said Mother. "Watch Peter, first."

Peter's dish-pan sled didn't travel like a real sled. It didn't go straight. It turned around and around. First Peter slid backwards, then sideways, then the dish pan whirled around again.

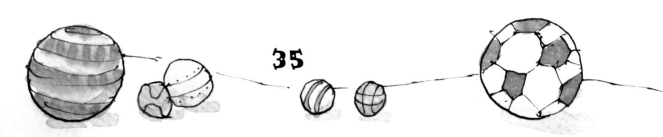

At last Peter reached the
bottom. He stood up,
looked around,
then he laughed.

"Did you like it?"
called Mother.

"I did!" cried Peter.
"It felt just like sliding
and rolling down hill at the
same time. I am going to play this
game all morning. Let's all go now."

"Very well," said Mother. "If you
bump into one another, it won't hurt
you. Get ready."

So the children climbed back up the
hill, then slid down again in their dish-
pan sleds. This time Polly bumped into

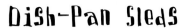

Tim, making him spin around and around, and he shouted all the way down. Polly went the rest of the way backwards, and at the bottom she fell out and lay in the snow, laughing.

Just then Wag-wag came running up the field. He was dragging Peter's real sled behind him. He had heard the children and was coming to find them. Perhaps he thought they had forgotten Peter's sled.

"Oh, look!" said Polly. "Wag-wag has a sled. Let's give him a slide. Come here, Wag-wag."

But Wag-wag wouldn't come. Instead, he ran up the hill past Mrs Howe. The children picked up their dish pans and chased him.

"Never mind," said Mother. "When he is tired of playing with the sled, he can bring it back or you can go after it. Now goodbye. Slide until the sun makes the crust soft, then come in. Do you like the new game?"

"Oh, we do, we do!" they all cried.

"And we like our new sleds, Mother. We are going to name them," said Polly.

"I am going to ask my mother to give me her dish pan," said Tim.

The children slid for a long time and got very hot and happy and snowy. At last the crust began to soften in the light of the sun. They started to sink in a little at every step.

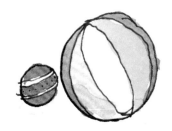

"I'll have one last slide," said Polly. "Then I'll go home."

"I'll just get my sled first," said Peter. "I wish Wag-wag had not left it so far away."

Peter started across the field. Before long, he came to a place where the snow was very soft. He sank into it as far as his legs could go. He could not get to the sled. So he went home feeling quite cross.

Tim's father was in the yard and his dog, Collie, was with him. Peter said, "Wag-wag left my sled out in the field and now the snow is soft and I cannot get to it."

Tim said, "My father will send Collie after your sled, Peter. Won't you, Father?"

"Oh, will you?" asked Peter. "I shall want to slide in the road after dinner. Dish pans

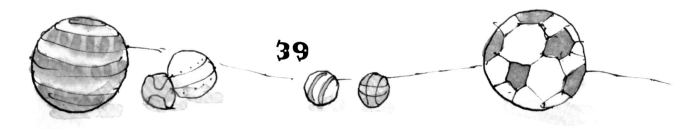

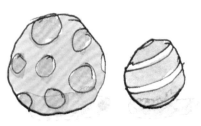

won't be any good in the road."

"Why, yes," said Tim's father. "Collie can get it. He will not break through the crust."

He showed Tim's sled to Collie, put the rope into Collie's mouth, and then pointed to the end of the big field. He said, "Collie, go bring the sled."

Collie went running over the snow. He found the sled and drew it home.

"There," said Tim, "I told you Collie is smarter than Wag-wag. He is, too."

"Maybe he isn't," said Peter. "Maybe Wag-wag was smart to leave my sled there. But I like Collie because he got it for me."